Praise for the Oi series:

'Delightfully mad'
Telegraph

'Gigglingly delightful'
Daily Mail

'This animal-rhyming silliness goes
from strength-to-strength'
Guardian

'Colourful, witty and silly'
BookTrust

To Jim, Sandy & Lola K.G.

Welcome to the world Stanley, Uncle Jim

HODDER CHILDREN'S BOOKS
First published in Great Britain in 2018
by Hodder and Stoughton

Text copyright © Kes Gray, 2018
Illustrations copyright © Jim Field, 2018

A CIP catalogue record for this book
is available from the British Library.

HB ISBN: 978 1 444 93732 9

10 9 8 7 6 5 4 3 2 1

Printed and bound in Italy

FSC
MIX
Paper from
responsible sources
FSC® C104740

Hodder Children's Books
An imprint of Hachette
Children's Group
Part of Hodder and Stoughton
Carmelite House
50 Victoria Embankment
London, EC4Y 0DZ

An Hachette UK Company
www.hachette.co.uk
www.hachettechildrens.co.uk

www.kesgray.com
www.jimfield.co.uk

Oi Duck-Billed Platypus!

Hodder
Children's
Books

Written by
Kes Gray

Illustrated by
Jim Field

"Oi Duck-Billed Platypus!

Sit on a ...

...

..."

"What about cluck-filled hatty bus?

Or yuk-spilled splatty mouse?

Or truck-frilled flappy goose?"

said the dog.

"**Don't be ridiculous,**" said the frog.

"Yes, don't be ridiculous,"
said the cat.

"I was only trying to help," said the dog.

"I'm waiting,"
said the duck-billed platypus.

"We're all waiting too,"
said a crowd of animals with
impossible-to-rhyme-with names.

"I know!" said the frog, "what's your **first** name?"

"Dolly," said the duck-billed platypus.

"Dollys sit on **brollies,"** smiled the frog.

"My first name is **Kate**,"
said the kookaburra.

"Kates sit on **gates,"** said the frog.

"My first name is **Herbert,**" said the hippopotamus.

"My first name is **Hannah,**" said the hedgehog.

"**Herberts** sit on **sherbets,**

Hannahs sit on **spanners,**

and **Jeans** sit on **baked beans,"** said the frog.

Lemonys sit on **anemones,**

Stellas sit on **propellers,**

BAKED BEANS

"He's good at this, isn't he?" said the dog.

"Too good," sighed the cat.

"What do **Ivanas** sit on?" asked the ibex.

"What about **Bobs?**" said the budgerigar.

"**Bobs** sit on **corn-on-the-cobs,**" said the frog.

"**Bobs** sit on corn-on-the-cobs,

Ozzies sit on cozzies,

Clives sit on hives,

Sophies sit on **trophies,**

Renatas sit on **chipolatas,**

and **Zanes** sit on **trains.**"

NUTS
ABOUT
NUTS
BY BRUCE & CYRIL

"How about **Niamhs?**" said the numbat.

"**Niamhs** sit on **leaves,**" said the frog.

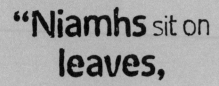

"**Niamhs** sit on
leaves,

Alices sit on
palaces,

Freddys
sit on
teddies,

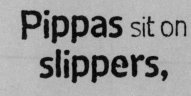

Pippas sit on
slippers,

Pauls sit on
walls,

Taylors
sit on
sailors,

and
Bayleys
sit on
ukeleles."

"That only leaves me," said the kangaroo.

"First name?" said the frog.

"Geraldine," said the kangaroo.

"Second name?"

"Jemima,"
said the kangaroo.

"Any other names?" asked the frog.

Amelia Esmerelda Honeydew Higginbottom-Pinkleponk-Johnson

said the kangaroo.